As Constant As the Stars

Written by Diane L. Nees
Illustrated by Janis A. Elsen

always reach for the stars
Diane L. Nees

Janis A. Elsen

PUBLISH AMERICA

PublishAmerica
Baltimore

First printing

Hardcover 9781462668861

PUBLISHED BY PUBLISHAMERICA, LLLP

www.publishamerica.com

Baltimore

Printed in the United States of America

Far to the east, through the Zep Galaxy and four billion steps past the third moon, Chi suspended himself in mid-air above the highest billowing branch of his favorite walla tree. He did his best thinking there.

"Son, it's time," his father called to him. "Waste is never a good thing."

"I didn't waste, father," Chi answered. "I ate all of my zookas... and the syrup, too," Chi added with a grin.

Chi's father, Aider, was the royal leader of their planet, Zeptune. Chi saw the look on his father's face and knew it better than anyone. It meant business. Aider smoothed his elbow fur for the fifth time that morning and Chi realized he was nervous about addressing the entire planet that day.

Being a royal leader must be a hard job, Chi thought.

"I was speaking about time, Chi. It's time for school. Good work makes one proud," Aider told him.

Chi sniffed the sweet crimson petals of the walla one more time before he ended his floatation and began his feet-first spiral descent. He landed at his father's side like any good meliken should.

"I'm on my way, Father. See you later. Tu-tu!"

"Tu-tu, my son." Aider's tentacles, normally stiff with concentration, wiggled and waggled when he smiled at his son. Chi waved as he hopped on his ziki and sped to...

the School of Astronomy where he was enrolled. Father said everything could be learned from the stars. Chi guessed he believed that was true. He only wished he could learn the way his father wanted him to.

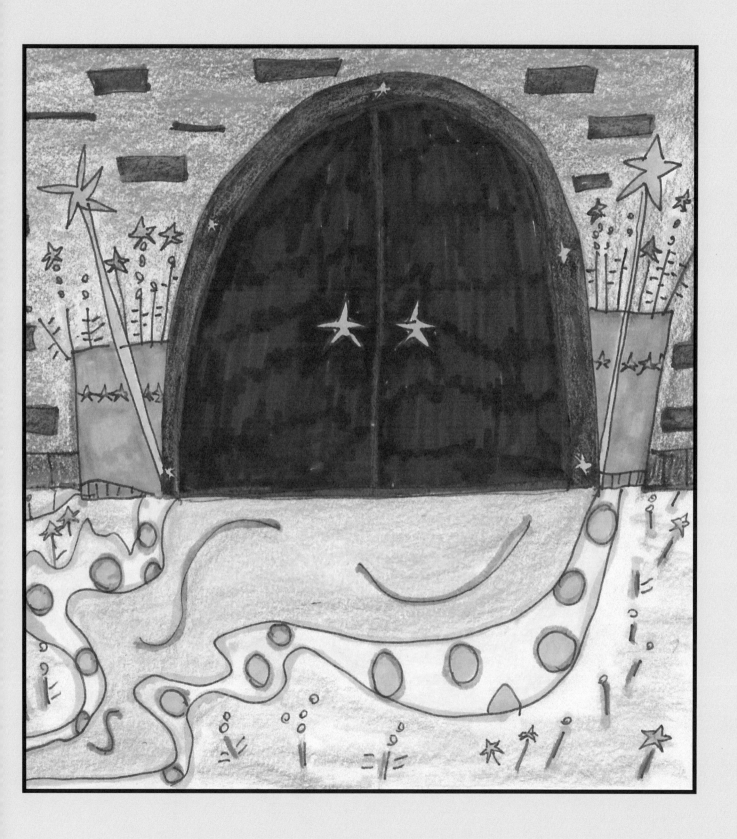

Sitting in class seemed hard. Chi was better at bouncing than sitting. He was better at singing than sitting.

And he was better at playing nano ball than sitting. In fact, he was better at anything than sitting!

He twisted, turned, wiggled and churned. Then he drooped, sighed, hummed, and rolled his eyes. Chi tried to listen but a bird chirped and a ziki zipped by.

He tried to make his father proud but the thoughts in his head buzzed around like bees on the walla blossoms.

But then Chi crumpled some paper and twisted his hair until finally his instructor, M. Zeery, asked, "Chi, are you with us? Do you plan to take this test like every other meliken here?"

"Test?" Chi could hardly say the word. His voice was lost in the air.

It was there on his desk... the test. Chi hadn't even noticed. The words looked wavy and everything he was supposed to know about the stars was lost in a blur. Perhaps if he was able to do his floatation above the walla tree he could think better.

He tried... and tried... and tried. Nothing. Chi wrote his name on the test but that was all. He looked at the clock, then his paper, then the clock, then his paper again. At quarter past a doandrum, Chi still had a blank test.

"Done, Chi?" M. Zeery questioned.

"I am," Chi told him softly as he handed the test in.

How could he face his father? He'd botched a test or two in his nine midyears but never had he turned in a blank test! Father said work would make him proud. His test was nothing to be proud of.

In Zeptune, one had to go to the garden of Zombowie at the exact darkest part of the eve and speak to the constellation, Aura, in person. If they wanted help, that is. And surely, Chi needed help.

Chi waited until the darkest hour, hopped on his ziki and sped to the garden. Blue stalks of thistle and bright yellow star flowers lined the path. Aura was not to be seen, only heard.

Chi stood alone in the black of the night and spilled his problem to Aura. He hoped for some answers.

"My child, you already know the answer," Aura spoke in a light echo.

"I will go back and take the test?" Chi guessed.

"That is to be seen."

"But what about my father? Will he know I tried?" Chi wanted to know.

"The answer is in the stars."

Chi wondered if his father had spoken to Aura first. He walked slowly home, steering his ziki along side of him. Chi was in no hurry. He knew the answer all right. Father would be angry... stomping angry! Father would have no patience for any son who turned in a blank test.

Chi tried his best to be quiet. He parked his ziki under his favorite walla and was just about to make a floatation when he noticed his father's shadow filter through the moonlight.

"My son is troubled." Father's voice drifted through the darkness. Aider slid next to Chi, hugging his side. He rested his furry arm around Chi's shoulders.

"Yes," Chi replied.

"M. Zeery talked to me."

Chi looked down. "I'm sorry. I know nothing about the stars like you want me to."

"Then, do you know about love?" Father asked.

Chi looked puzzled, then nodded. "Yes, you will love me if you are proud. I will ask M. Zeery to retake the test."

"Proud comes from within. That's how it should be. But I will be more than snappered with pleasure that you have decided how to solve your problem. That will give us both a warm feeling."

"Love?" Chi asked.

"Love is an always thing and, yes, very warm," Father answered. He snuggled even closer to Chi and raised his arm, pointing out into the galaxy.

"I'll tell you something, Chi. Stars are a constant in life. They embrace the night with their brilliance. Even though moon cycles might hide their presence, they are always there. Do you understand, son?"

Chi's nod was weak, so Aider went on. "Love does the same. A cover of worry might disguise the feeling but it will always win out! Love shines though, as it should. Do you see?"

Chi reached up and hugged his father tight.

"I do, Father. Stars weather any storm. They always light the way... like love." There was a twinkle from above.

"Always," Father said, returning Chi's embrace.

Would you like to see your manuscript become a book?

If you are interested in becoming a PublishAmerica author, please submit your manuscript for possible publication to us at:

acquisitions@publishamerica.com

You may also mail in your manuscript to:

**PublishAmerica
PO Box 151
Frederick, MD 21705**

___

We also offer free graphics for Children's Picture Books!

___

www.publishamerica.com

CPSIA information can be obtained
at www.ICGtesting.com
Printed in the USA
LVIW012055170612

286208LV00002BA